The Little Forest

Elf Oak W...

Gaston's Cave

Elf Windmill

Little Castle

Great El...

The Meadow

Mrs Witch's House

Royal Golf Course

Frog Pond

N
W E
S

The Bramble Woods

The Pine Forest

# Ben Elf's Birthday

This adventure starts at The Great Elf Tree . . .

Today, it is Ben Elf's birthday.
"Happy birthday, Ben!" cheer Mr and Mrs Elf.
"Thanks, Mum. Thanks, Dad," cries Ben.
Just then, the doorbell rings and Ben runs downstairs to see who it is.

It's Holly the fairy princess.

"Hi, Holly," gasps Ben. "You're early for my party.

Have you brought me a card?"

"Er . . ." stutters Holly, confused.

"Holly!" says Ben. "You haven't forgotten my birthday, have you?"

"Happy birthday, Ben," cries Holly. "I've just got to pop home. Bye!"

Holly flies home to the Little Castle, so she can make Ben a card.
She tries to use one of Nanny Plum's magic spells to make it, but she's
not sure of the words.

**"Hocus pocus, plinkity plonk. Er . . .**

**Make me a birthday card, super duper quick!"**

Holly's magic wand twinkles and the paintbrushes lift up into the air.

Meanwhile, Nanny Plum is busy helping King Thistle.

"Nanny, can you do a magic spell to make me comfortable?" he asks.

"Oh King Thistle, you lazy thing. You could do a spell yourself," she replies.

"But my wand is over there," moans the king. So Nanny Plum uses a spell to put King Thistle in a very comfortable invisible chair!

BOOM!

Back in the kitchen, Holly wants
the paintbrushes to hurry up.
"I'll do a stronger spell to make
you go faster!" cries Holly,
waving her wand.

"Zam! Pop! Zip! Pow!
More! Bigger! Faster! Now!"
BOOM! Suddenly, everything grows very big and rises
up into the air.
"Naannnyyy!" shouts Holly. "Help! Help!"

"Goodness me," gasps Nanny Plum, finding Holly and the whole kitchen covered in paint. "I must stop this, now."

"Thunder and lightning,
North winds blow.
Magic spells away you go!"
Everything falls back to the ground with a big **CRASH!**

The kitchen is still covered in paint, but the magic has stopped. "Thank you, Nanny," cries Holly, very relieved. "You stopped it." "Yes," replies Nanny Plum, "but I had to stop all the fairy magic in the whole of the castle." Just then, there is a loud **BANG** from upstairs . . .

King Thistle has fallen down on the ground. Nanny Plum, Holly and the rest of the royal family run up to see what happened.

"Oof! What happened to the magic?" he asks.

"Ahem," begins Nanny Plum. "There was a little problem and I had to stop all the fairy magic in the castle for one day. Sorry, your majesty!"

Suddenly, the fairy on the TV speaks, "And the weather in the Little Kingdom today will be bright and sunny . . ."
"Hang on," gasps King Thistle, "if you've stopped the magic, why is the TV working?"

"Er, the TV's not magic, your majesty," replies Nanny Plum.
"Isn't it? Really?" says the King, somewhat surprised.

Now, Holly has to make Ben's birthday card without any spells.
"This is going to be fun," giggles Holly.
"I think I'll start with a picture of Ben!"
Holly paints a wonderful picture and finishes it off with sparkly glitter.

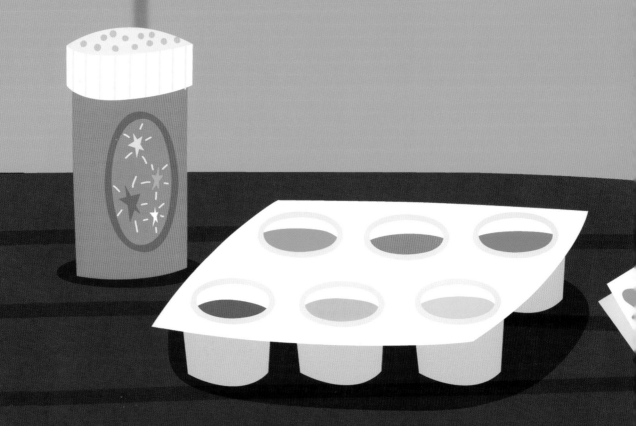

"It's amazing what can be done without using magic," says Nanny Plum. "Now quick Holly, or you'll be late for Ben's birthday party!"

Holly arrives at Ben's birthday party and gives him his card.
"It isn't very good," she says. "I made it myself."
"You didn't use magic?" asks Ben. "It looks fantastic, thank you!"
Later on, Holly confesses to Ben, "I did forget your birthday."
"I know," says Ben. "You always do! But it doesn't matter, you're still my best friend."